For Lorie Ann, Anna, Julie, Kristen,
Paul, George, Barbara, and Emily —J. H.

To Jan, for innumerable reasons —T. L.

Henry Holt and Company, LLC
Publishers since 1866
175 Fifth Avenue, New York, New York 10010
mackids.com

Library of Congress Cataloging-in-Publication Data
Holub, Joan.
Zero the hero / by Joan Holub ; illustrated by Tom Lichtenheld. — 1st ed.
p.   cm.
"Christy Ottaviano Books."
Summary: Zero believes that he is a hero, but the counting numbers think
he is worthless until they get into trouble with some Roman numerals,
and only Zero can help.
ISBN 978-0-8050-9384-1 (hc)
[1. Zero (The number)—Fiction. 2. Numbers, Natural—Fiction. 3. Heroes—
Fiction. 4. Humorous stories.] I. Lichtenheld, Tom, ill. II. Title.
PZ7.H7427Zer 2012   [E]—dc22   2011012900

First Edition—2012

The illustrations are rendered in ink, pastel, and colored pencil.
Printed in China by Macmillan Production Asia, Ltd.,
Kowloon Bay, Hong Kong
(Vendor Code: 10)

10 9 8 7 6 5

ZERO the HERO

Joan Holub & Tom Lichtenheld

A BOOK ABOUT NOTHING!

Christy Ottaviano Books   HENRY HOLT AND COMPANY • NEW YORK

Unlike most numbers, Zero believed himself to be a hero.
He just needed a chance to prove it.

But Zero's belief in himself didn't count for much when it came to fitting in.

In order to amount to anything, Zero had to
stand in the shadow of others more glamorous than he was.

Occasionally, he was mistaken for
various circular objects, seemingly at random.
Some days, it really got to him.

When it came to addition, he was virtually invisible.
Other numbers seemed to pass right through him.
Almost like magic.

The same thing happened with subtraction.
In their frustration, some numbers were unkind.

Turns out, Zero stunk even more at division. So badly, in fact, that other numbers simply refused to be divided by him at all.

Still, his belief in his wonderfulness persisted.
Then one day, during multiplication, it was discovered that
any number times Zero equals—you guessed it!—Zero.

Fearing extinction, the others ran from him.
Who could blame them?

As the others scurried away, Zero had a horrible realization. A real superhero wouldn't multiply his friends into nothingness. That's the kind of stuff only an evil villain would do.

Could it be that he wasn't a hero at all?

The thought gave Zero a hollow feeling inside.

His confidence shaken,
he tucked himself tight and rolled away . . .

. . . heading for infinity
or oblivion, whichever came first.

The counting numbers didn't even notice Zero was gone.

That is, until they encountered unexpected story problems.

To take their minds off their problems,
they tried playing a game of round-off.
But this proved impossible without Zero.

No question, the counting numbers were missing their friend.

In fact, they were so busy missing him that they didn't notice they were being surrounded.

Before the numbers knew it,
they had been captured . . . by Roman soldiers!

1, 2, 3, 4, 5, 6, 7, 8, and 9 were tossed into the gladiator ring.

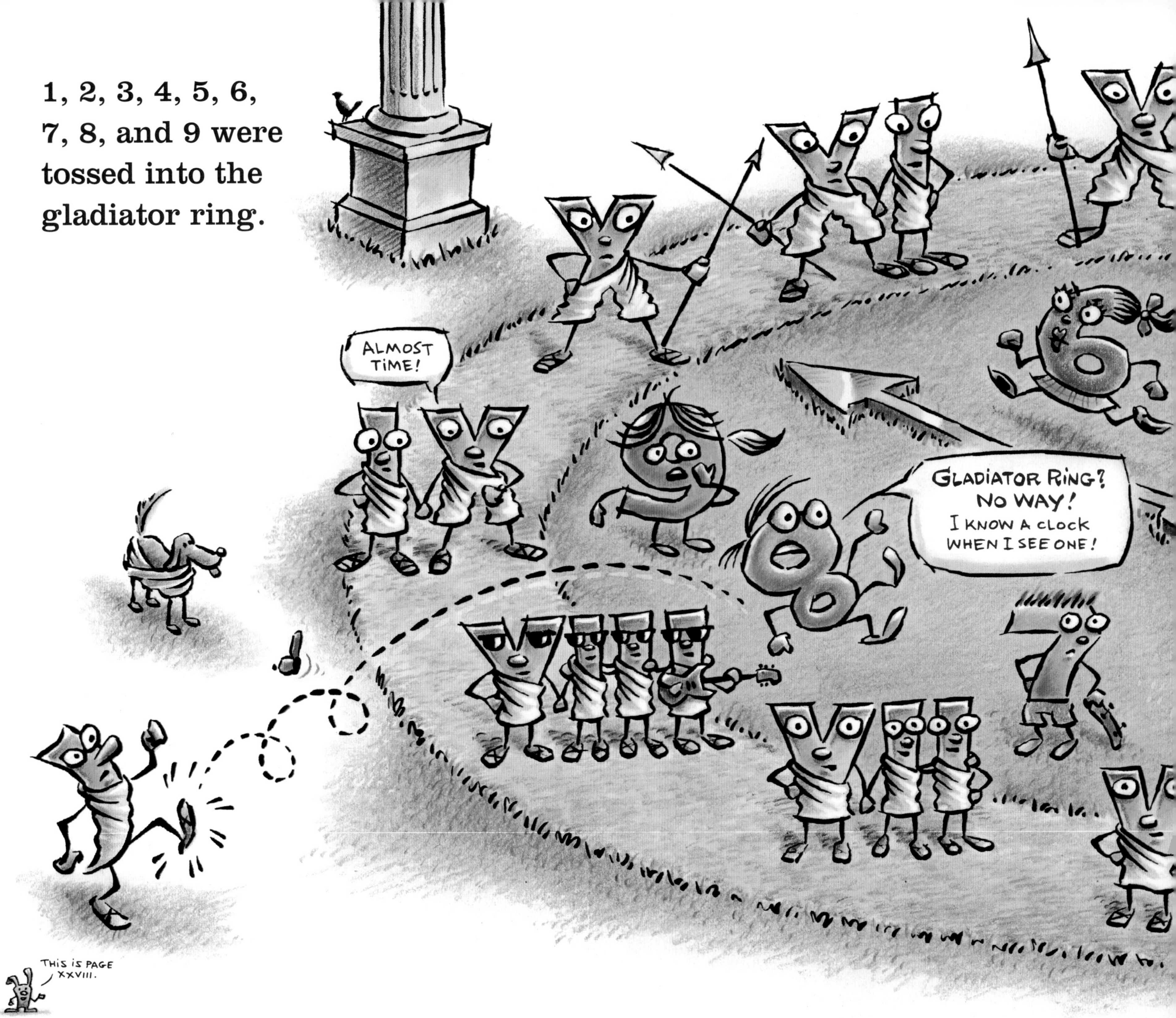

The Roman soldiers were counting the minutes until they'd attack!

It was a time of darkness and despair.

From far away, Zero heard his pals call for help.

This is a job for Zero the Hero,
he thought.

Faster than a speeding donut, Zero zoomed to the rescue.

"Release the numbers or else!"
Zero told the Romans.

"Or else what?"
the Romans replied.

"Or else I will unleash
a force greater than you can imagine—the power of nothing!"

"Go ahead," said the Romans. "We're not afraid of nothing."

Left no choice, Zero grabbed a nearby rock and proceeded
to demonstrate his amazing power.

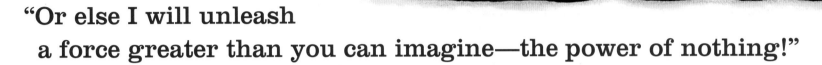

When the Roman numerals saw the rock disappear, they decided to disappear, too.

They ran away as fast as they could.

"All hail Zero the Hero!"
shouted the counting numbers.
"Thank you for saving us!"

With his friends around him once more,
and the knowledge that he had fought evil and won,
Zero no longer felt empty inside.

Now that hollow nothingness inside him
was filled with something.

And that something was . . .

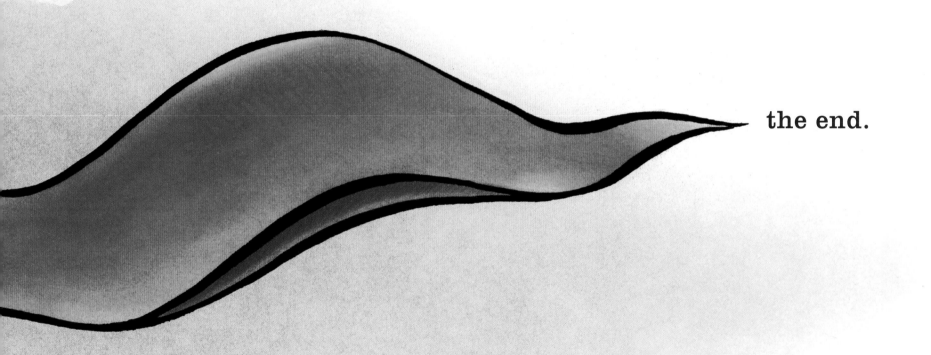

the end.